This book belongs to:

_____

PENGUIN YOUNG READERS LICENSES
An imprint of Penguin Random House LLC, New York

First published in the United States of America by Penguin Young Readers Licenses,
an imprint of Penguin Random House LLC, New York, 2022

Copyright © 2022 by Cosmic Kids Brands Limited
COSMIC KIDS ™ and the Cosmic Kids logo are trademarks
of Cosmic Kids Brands Limited

Penguin supports copyright. Copyright fuels creativity, encourages
diverse voices, promotes free speech, and creates a vibrant culture.
Thank you for buying an authorized edition of this book and for complying
with copyright laws by not reproducing, scanning, or distributing any part
of it in any form without permission. You are supporting writers
and allowing Penguin to continue to publish books for every reader.

Visit us online at penguinrandomhouse.com.

Manufactured in China

ISBN 9780593386866   10 9 8 7 6 5 4 3 2 1 HH

Lettering by Ellen Duda
Design by Taylor Abatiell

We made this book for

YOU!

It's your friend,
your guide,
and something you
can turn to whenever
you need.

It will always be
here for you.

COSMIC KIDS!

TODAY I WILL BE...

A Daily MINDFULNESS Journal

How to Use the Daily Track

Every day, in the morning and evening, write or draw how you feel and what you did that day!

Every few days, you will be getting a new challenge in your daily track! Have fun!

—/—/—

DAILY TRACK

MORNING

Today I want to be:

≡ Brave! ≡

Today I want to:

- ★ Learn a language
- ★ Do something nice for someone
- ★ Hug my dog

EVENING

Today I felt:

Excited!

Today I:

- ★ Finished reading a book
- ★ Hugged my dog
- ★ Learned a new yoga pose

___ / ___ / ___

DAILY TRACK
MORNING

Today I want to be:

Today I want to:

EVENING

Today I felt:

Today I:

__ / __ / __

DAILY TRACK
MORNING

Today I want to be:

Today I want to:

EVENING

Today I felt:

Today I:

___ / ___ / ___

DAILY TRACK
MORNING

Today I want to be:

Today I want to:

EVENING

Today I felt:

Today I:

__ / __ / __

DAILY TRACK
MORNING

Today I want to be:

Today I want to:

EVENING

Today I felt:

Today I:

—/—/—

DAILY TRACK

MORNING

What do you think about as you get ready to start the day? Do you make a list of things you want to do or have a goal you want to achieve? Write or draw your goals!

EVENING

What do you think about when you get ready for bed? Are you already thinking about tomorrow? Try focusing on your breathing—slowing it down and counting your breaths. Do this a few times and write or draw how you feel.

—/—/—

DAILY TRACK
MORNING

Today I want to be:

Today I want to:

EVENING

Today I felt:

Today I:

__ / __ / __

DAILY TRACK
MORNING

Today I want to be:

Today I want to:

EVENING

Today I felt:

Today I:

YOGA POSES
Good Morning!

Time to get ready for the day! Try out these yoga poses so your body can wake up with you!

Hello Sun Pose

Tree Pose

Dog Pose

Mouse Pose

DAILY TRACK

MORNING

Write or draw three things you would like to do today.

EVENING

What surprised you about today? Write or draw it out!

___/___/___

DAILY TRACK
MORNING

Today I want to be:

Today I want to:

EVENING

Today I felt:

Today I:

— / — / —

DAILY TRACK
MORNING

Today I want to be:

Today I want to:

EVENING

Today I felt:

Today I:

— / — / —

DAILY TRACK
MORNING

Today I want to be:

Today I want to:

EVENING

Today I felt:

Today I:

_ _ / _ _ / _ _

DAILY TRACK
MORNING

Today I want to be:

Today I want to:

EVENING

Today I felt:

Today I:

___ / ___ / ___

DAILY TRACK
MORNING

Today I want to be:

Today I want to:

EVENING

Today I felt:

Today I:

— / — / —

DAILY TRACK
MORNING

Today I want to be:

Today I want to:

EVENING

Today I felt:

Today I:

YOGA POSES

Good Evening!

The day is done, and it's time to wind down and relax. Try out these yoga poses and think about all that you've accomplished today.

Magic Carpet Pose

Lake Pose

Treasure Chest Pose

Eye Cupping Pose

_ _ / _ _ / _ _

DAILY TRACK
MORNING

Today I want to be:

Today I want to:

EVENING

Today I felt:

Today I:

DAILY TRACK

MORNING

Today is a great day to learn something new! Write or draw three things you would like to try or just learn today.

EVENING

Did you try or learn something new today? Write or draw it on this page!

___ / ___ / ___

DAILY TRACK
MORNING

Today I want to be:

Today I want to:

EVENING

Today I felt:

Today I:

___ / ___ / ___

DAILY TRACK

MORNING

Today I want to be:

Today I want to:

EVENING

Today I felt:

Today I:

—/—/—

DAILY TRACK
MORNING

Today I want to be:

Today I want to:

EVENING

Today I felt:

Today I:

__ / __ / __

DAILY TRACK
MORNING

Today I want to be:

Today I want to:

EVENING

Today I felt:

Today I:

___ / ___ / ___

DAILY TRACK
MORNING

Today I want to be:

Today I want to:

EVENING

Today I felt:

Today I:

MENTAL CLEANUP

Let's clean up! Write, draw, or even glue pictures
(with help from your parents!) that show how you're
feeling. By putting everything down on this page,
we're able to look at our feelings, understand why
we feel the way we feel, and accept them.

—_/_—/_—

DAILY TRACK
MORNING

Today I want to be:

Today I want to:

EVENING

Today I felt:

Today I:

— / — / —

DAILY TRACK
MORNING

Write or draw the five things you notice as soon as you wake up. Is it the sun on your cheek? The sound of your alarm clock? The smell of breakfast being made?

EVENING

Write or draw five things you notice as you get ready for bed. The glow of your lamp on the bedside table? The sound of your parents getting ready for bed?

_ / _ / _

DAILY TRACK
MORNING

Today I want to be:

Today I want to:

EVENING

Today I felt:

Today I:

__/__/__

DAILY TRACK
MORNING

Today I want to be:

Today I want to:

EVENING

Today I felt:

Today I:

___ / ___ / ___

DAILY TRACK

MORNING

Today I want to be:

Today I want to:

EVENING

Today I felt:

Today I:

— / — / —

DAILY TRACK
MORNING

Today I want to be:

Today I want to:

EVENING

Today I felt:

Today I:

— / — / —

DAILY TRACK
MORNING

Today I want to be:

Today I want to:

EVENING

Today I felt:

Today I:

YOGA POSES

Feeling Sad? That's Okay

It's okay to feel sad. So is having a good cry! Whenever you're done feeling down, let's do some yoga poses to help you feel better and calmer.

Monkey Jumps

Mermaid Pose

Camel Pose

Happy Baby Pose

—/—/—

DAILY TRACK
MORNING

Today I want to be:

Today I want to:

EVENING

Today I felt:

Today I:

—/—/—

DAILY TRACK
MORNING

Today I want to be:

Today I want to:

EVENING

Today I felt:

Today I:

DAILY TRACK

MORNING

What are three things you're proud of? Write or draw them.
Don't worry if they're small things!

EVENING

What are three things you did today that you're proud of?
It can be that you learned a new word, taught your dog how
to sit, or even helped someone today! Write or draw them on
this page!

___ / ___ / ___

DAILY TRACK
MORNING

Today I want to be:

Today I want to:

EVENING

Today I felt:

Today I:

DAILY TRACK

MORNING

Today I want to be:

Today I want to:

EVENING

Today I felt:

Today I:

__ / __ / __

DAILY TRACK
MORNING

Today I want to be:

Today I want to:

EVENING

Today I felt:

Today I:

— / — / —

DAILY TRACK
MORNING

Today I want to be:

Today I want to:

EVENING

Try the yoga exercise on the following page and write how you feel afterward!

MINDFULNESS EXERCISE

How to Meditate

Are you worried about a test?
Do you get nervous when you go somewhere new?
Let's practice meditating! Meditation is a great way
to help us clear our minds and calm our nerves.
Let's try it!

*Here's a tip! Try setting a timer for five minutes for
this exercise. That way you'll know how long to do it.*

1. Sit tall and proud like a king or queen
2. Close your eyes
3. Take slow, deep breaths
4. Focus on your breathing

Be kind to yourself! Don't worry if your mind jumps
around like a monkey–it happens to everyone! Simply
notice it, come back, and focus on your breathing.
And when you're done, write how you feel after
doing the exercise!

DAILY TRACK
MORNING

Today I want to be:

Today I want to:

EVENING

Today I felt:

Today I:

DAiLY TRACK

MORNiNG

We all have worries. They're perfectly normal! By writing them down you're giving your mind a place to put them.

EVENiNG

Did any of those worries you were having cause a problem today? If they did, how did you solve it? Did you realize that some of those worries weren't actually likely to come true? If so, maybe you don't need to worry about them anymore!

__ / __ / __

DAILY TRACK
MORNING

Today I want to be:

Today I want to:

EVENING

Today I felt:

Today I:

___ / ___ / ___

DAILY TRACK
MORNING

Today I want to be:

Today I want to:

EVENING

Today I felt:

Today I:

___/___/___

DAILY TRACK
MORNING

Today I want to be:

Today I want to:

EVENING

Today I felt:

Today I:

—/—/—

DAILY TRACK
MORNING

Today I want to be:

Today I want to:

EVENING

Today I felt:

Today I:

__ / __ / __

DAILY TRACK
MORNING

Today I want to be:

Today I want to:

EVENING

Today I felt:

Today I:

COLORING

DAILY TRACK

MORNING

Today I want to be:

Today I want to:

EVENING

Today I felt:

Today I:

— / — / —

DAILY TRACK
MORNING

Write or draw three things you would like to do today.

EVENING

What surprised you about today? Write or draw it out!

—/—/—

DAILY TRACK

MORNING

Today I want to be:

Today I want to:

EVENING

Today I felt:

Today I:

__ / __ / __

DAILY TRACK
MORNING

Today I want to be:

Today I want to:

EVENING

Today I felt:

Today I:

DAILY TRACK

_ / _ / _

MORNING

Today I want to be:

Today I want to:

EVENING

Today I felt:

Today I:

—/—/—

DAILY TRACK
MORNING

Today I want to be:

Today I want to:

EVENING

Today I felt:

Today I:

__ / __ / __

DAILY TRACK
MORNING

Today I want to be:

Today I want to:

EVENING

Today I felt:

Today I:

YOGA POSES
to Help Beat Nerves

Fun fact! Nerves come from the same place as excitement in our minds, but sometimes our nerves get a little overwhelmed, and that's okay! As you try these yoga poses, try to reframe those feelings to help you settle your nerves while still making the most of the power inside you.

Ear Rubbing Pose

Butterfly Pose

Tumble Dryer Pose

Squat Pose

_ / _ / _

DAILY TRACK
MORNING

Today I want to be:

Today I want to:

EVENING

Today I felt:

Today I:

___ / ___ / ___

DAILY TRACK
MORNING

Today I want to be:

Today I want to:

EVENING

Today I felt:

Today I:

DAILY TRACK

MORNING

Today I want to be:

Today I want to:

EVENING

Today I felt:

Today I:

DAILY TRACK
MORNING

Dance time! Let's get pumped up! What's your favorite song and how does it make you feel? Write or draw it on the page!

EVENING

Time to wind down for the night. What song do you listen to when you're getting ready for bed?

___/___/___

DAILY TRACK
MORNING

Today I want to be:

Today I want to:

EVENING

Today I felt:

Today I:

___ / ___ / ___

DAILY TRACK
MORNING

Today I want to be:

Today I want to:

EVENING

Today I felt:

Today I:

—/—/—

DAILY TRACK
MORNING

Today I want to be:

Today I want to:

EVENING

Today I felt:

Today I:

TUNE IN TO YOUR SENSES

Sometimes we get so busy and have so much to do that we forget that it's also important to give our minds a break. Remember that it's okay to sit and focus on yourself! Being in a place of noticing rather than doing is a great practice for life! Let's try it.

Get nice and comfy and focus on your breathing. When you're ready, notice what is around you. You can even close your eyes if you want! That way, you can use your other senses like sound and touch to notice new things.

When you're done, write or draw what you've noticed on this page!

__ / __ / __

DAILY TRACK

MORNING

Today I want to be:

Today I want to:

EVENING

Today I felt:

Today I:

_ _ / _ _ / _ _

DAILY TRACK
MORNING

Today I want to be:

Today I want to:

EVENING

Today I felt:

Today I:

— / — / —

DAILY TRACK

MORNING

Today I want to be:

Today I want to:

EVENING

Today I felt:

Today I:

__ / __ / __

DAILY TRACK
MORNING

What are your favorite things to do outside? Write or draw them out! Use your senses (touch, sight, smell, sound, taste) to help you.

EVENING

What was the highlight of your day? Write or draw it out! Use your senses to help you.

—/—/—

DAILY TRACK
MORNING

Today I want to be:

Today I want to:

EVENING

Today I felt:

Today I:

— / — / —

DAILY TRACK
MORNING

Today I want to be:

Today I want to:

EVENING

Today I felt:

Today I:

__ / __ / __

DAiLY TRACK
MORNiNG

Today I want to be:

Today I want to:

EVENiNG

Today I felt:

Today I:

GRATITUDE

Gratitude is a great way to power up on feelings of happiness and well-being. Write down a list of things you are grateful for. It can be anything!
A hug from your parents or the fresh, clean air. Whenever you're having a tough day, you can look at this list and remember that things will always be okay and that there are always things to be happy about!

_ / _ / _

DAILY TRACK
MORNING

Today I want to be:

Today I want to:

EVENING

Today I felt:

Today I:

___ / ___ / ___

DAILY TRACK
MORNING

Today I want to be:

Today I want to:

EVENING

Today I felt:

Today I:

—/—/—

DAILY TRACK

MORNING

What are your favorite things to do inside? Describe them using your five senses (touch, sight, smell, sound, taste)!

EVENING

What was something new you learned today that you didn't know before?

_ _ / _ _ / _ _

DAILY TRACK
MORNING

Today I want to be:

Today I want to:

EVENING

Today I felt:

Today I:

— / — / —

DAILY TRACK

MORNING

Today I want to be:

Today I want to:

EVENING

Today I felt:

Today I:

— / — / —

DAILY TRACK
MORNING

Today I want to be:

Today I want to:

EVENING

Today I felt:

Today I:

__ / __ / __

DAILY TRACK
MORNING

Today I want to be:

Today I want to:

EVENING

Today I felt:

Today I:

AFFIRMATION

Top tip! Affirmations work even better when we say them out loud. When you say it, you make it real! Which makes it more likely to work! Let's try it!

Today I will:

BE BRAVE

DECIDE TO BE KIND

TRY SOMETHING NEW

LISTEN BEFORE I SPEAK

—— / —— / ——

DAILY TRACK
MORNING

Today I want to be:

Today I want to:

EVENING

Today I felt:

Today I:

__ / __ / __

DAILY TRACK
MORNING

Today I want to be:

Today I want to:

EVENING

Today I felt:

Today I:

DAILY TRACK

MORNING

Draw a picture of yourself doing your favorite activity!

EVENING

Draw a picture of yourself doing your favorite activity as you get ready for bed!

— / — / —

DAILY TRACK
MORNING

Today I want to be:

Today I want to:

EVENING

Today I felt:

Today I:

_ / _ / _

DAILY TRACK
MORNING

Today I want to be:

Today I want to:

EVENING

Today I felt:

Today I:

—/—/—

DAILY TRACK
MORNING

Today I want to be:

Today I want to:

EVENING

Today I felt:

Today I:

_ / _ / _

DAILY TRACK
MORNING

Today I want to be:

Today I want to:

EVENING

Today I felt:

Today I:

YOGA POSES
to Feel Like a Warrior

Sometimes you need to dig deep and find strength to help yourself deal with day-to-day challenges. You DO have the power within you . . . and sometimes it goes to sleep! So let's wake it up and see what happens!

Dinosaur Pose

Hero Pose

Surfer-Warrior Pose

Wolf Pose

— / — / —

DAILY TRACK
MORNING

Today I want to be:

Today I want to:

EVENING

Today I felt:

Today I:

— / — / —

DAILY TRACK
MORNING

Think of three strong words that will help you today.

EVENING

Think of three words that describe how your day went.

_ / _ / _

DAILY TRACK

MORNING

Today I want to be:

Today I want to:

EVENING

Today I felt:

Today I:

__ / __ / __

DAILY TRACK
MORNING

Today I want to be:

Today I want to:

EVENING

Today I felt:

Today I:

___ / ___ / ___

DAILY TRACK

MORNING

Today I want to be:

Today I want to:

EVENING

Today I felt:

Today I:

_ _ / _ _ / _ _

DAILY TRACK
MORNING

Today I want to be:

Today I want to:

EVENING

Today I felt:

Today I:

___ / ___ / ___

DAILY TRACK
MORNING

Today I want to be:

Today I want to:

EVENING

Today I felt:

Today I:

WELL DONE!

Now what's next?

As you look at all the things you accomplished in this journal, think about what you want to do in the future.

Turn the page to **write** or **draw** what you want to do with everything that you have learned!

Cosmic Kids is on a mission to make yoga and mindfulness fun for kids. In 2012, wife and husband team Jaime and Martin Amor filmed their first "yoga adventure" in their local sports and social club. Now Cosmic Kids Yoga has three hundred million views on YouTube, a huge library of entertaining, high-quality video content which helps kids enjoy moving, develop self-regulation skills, and increase their wellness. Thousands of adults have learned how to teach yoga to kids in their communities via their kids yoga teacher training programs, too. Jaime, the presenter of Cosmic Kids, is renowned for her ability to empathize and communicate with children and has been variously described as "America's de facto phys ed teacher" (*Washington Post*), "a digital sensation" (*Wall Street Journal*), and "a modern day Mary Poppins" (*Washington Post*).